THE CURSE OF HEARTWOOD ACADEMY

MARTY CHAN

orca soundings

ORCA BOOK PUBLISHERS

Published in Canada and the United States in 2026 by Orca Book Publishers.

Library and Archives Canada Cataloguing in Publication
Title: The curse of Heartwood Academy / Marty Chan.
Names: Chan, Marty, author
Series: Orca soundings.
Description: Series statement: Orca soundings
Identifiers: Canadiana (print) 20250162512 | Canadiana (ebook) 20250162520 | ISBN 9781459841895 (softcover) | ISBN 9781459841901 (PDF) | ISBN 9781459841918 (EPUB)
Subjects: LCGFT: Novels.
Classification: LCC PS8555.H39244 C87 2026 | DDC jC813/.54—dc23

Library of Congress Control Number: 2025932569

Summary: In this high-interest accessible novel for teen readers, fifteen-year-old Allie Lau finds herself pursued by some kind of ghoul when she disturbs a grave during a school hazing ritual.

Orca Book Publishers is committed to reducing the consumption of nonrenewable resources in the production of our books. We make every effort to use materials that support a sustainable future.

Orca Book Publishers gratefully acknowledges the support for its publishing programs provided by the following agencies: the Government of Canada, the Canada Council for the Arts and the Province of British Columbia through the BC Arts Council and the Book Publishing Tax Credit.

Design by Ella Collier.
Cover illustration by shutterstock.com/elf.illus and shutterstock.com/macrovector
Edited by Gabrielle Prendergast.
Author photo by Ryan Parker.

Printed and bound in Canada.

29 28 27 26 • 1 2 3 4

CERTIFIED CANADIAN PUBLISHER

ORCA BOOK PUBLISHERS
orcabook.com

Chapter One

“My new school is a horror movie” was the last thing I expected to see on my bingo card. Heartwood Academy was supposed to be one of the country’s best boarding schools, with students coming from around the world. But my first thought about the place was, Where does the *head* vampire live? The old, ivy-covered brick buildings reminded me of the creepy castles in the classic horror films my grandpa watched.

I stood on the lush green lawn and stared at a three-story L-shaped building. A redbrick tower rose from the roof where the two sections met. As I gazed at the white-trimmed windows and the ugly winged statues on top of the steep roof, a shudder ran through my entire body. *Did my parents even see this place before they signed me up?* My brothers and sister didn't have to attend boarding school. Why had I been singled out for this punishment? Mom claimed I had a talent that only Heartwood Academy could bring out, but I figured this was code for *I can't handle my daughter. Someone take her off my hands.*

"This is where all your classes will be held," our tour guide announced to the group of kids standing next to me.

Pru Cotton was her name. She was a senior student and a one-person welcoming committee. She wore the Heartwood uniform—a forest-green jacket and skirt. The school crest was stitched on her jacket pocket—three clasped hands against the backdrop of a heart. Her blond hair bounced with natural curls. She was so different than me. I was more of a slob with my ragged jeans and T-shirt. I wondered if I could get curly hair like hers, but I had the same hair as my Chinese dad. Straight, stiff and black. Well, I probably had more of it than he did.

"The third floor is where you'll find the offices. Your classes will be on the main and second floors," Pru said. She pointed to the shorter section of the L shape. "And that's where you'll find the cafeteria and gym. Any questions?"

"Why is this place so creepy?" I asked.

Pru cracked a smug grin. "What's your name?"

"Allie. Allie Lau," I answered, tapping the name tag on my chest.

"So, Allie, do you find Heartwood Academy unsettling?"

I nodded, as did most of the kids around me.

I could see Pru loved this. She breathed in, letting silence fall. Then she leaned forward and whispered, "The founder of the school was Claude Dubois. He made a fortune in construction, and he had no plans to spend any of it on something like a school. His money and all that came with it was meant for his family yet to be. He and his wife, Margaret, were expecting their first child. But fate had other plans. Margaret Dubois died giving birth to a daughter. They say that the child lived only as long as a few heartbeats, then joined her mother in the hereafter. Shattered, Claude wanted to honor his wife, so he turned his estate into Heartwood Academy."

I shrugged. "Why a school?"

Pru eyed me up and down. "You're a curious cat, Allie. Good question. Some say Margaret Dubois was a teacher, and Claude wanted to honor her memory with a school. But I heard she was into the dark arts and talked to spirits from the beyond. Claude wanted to erase that part of her life with Heartwood."

"Really?" a boy in the back asked.

Pru nodded. "After Margaret died, Claude hoped the students would fill the empty spot left by his wife's and daughter's deaths. But something else filled Claude's heart. A spirit Margaret may have contacted when she was carrying their child."

Pru paused and surveyed our reactions.

What a drama queen.

She continued, "Claude couldn't bear to live without his family. His broken heart couldn't be fixed no matter how many students walked the Heartwood halls."

Pru pointed to the tower rising from the third-floor roof.

"They say that despair took Claude to the top of the school. He leapt off to join his wife and child in the hereafter. But there are a few who believe he didn't take his own life. They believe that whatever spirit Margaret contacted caused the deaths of all three Dubois. Some think that spirit is still here."

She let her last statement hang in the air as she glanced at the forest next to the school grounds. The kids around me shuffled their feet nervously, glancing around the buildings.

"Let's continue our tour," Pru said.

We headed along the cobblestone path toward another set of buildings situated near the forest that butted up against the school grounds. I was used to living in a city where you'd only find trees in fenced-off parks. Maybe the odd tree on a sidewalk, but definitely not a forest growing right next to all the buildings. Add in Pru's story about the Dubois family, and this had the makings of a horror movie. The only thing we needed to make it complete was a gruesome discovery.

"Ahhhhhhhhhhhhh!" Pru shrieked. "What is that?"

She pointed to the edge of the woods.

Chapter Two

Pru rushed to the trees, and we followed. She stopped at the edge of the woods and looked down at a lump on the ground. A dead raccoon. Its cold, unblinking eyes stared up. They bothered me more than the animal's twisted body. Its head was bent at an odd angle to its neck. Tufts of fur had been yanked out. Dried blood was splattered across the edges of the hole in its chest. The raccoon's tiny claws reached upward as if begging for mercy.

Though the body was half-rotted, the only smell came from the pine trees around us. Strange, I thought. This thing should be ripe by now.

My fellow students stood beside me, staring at the grim sight. As I scanned the pale faces of my schoolmates, I wondered if we shared the same question: Is this really our first day of boarding school?

"This was the ghoul's work," Pru said. She paused for dramatic effect and scanned the pale faces of the students standing around the body.

"Who's the ghoul?" I asked.

A few of the other new students muttered the same question.

Pru held up a finger to silence us.

She was acting like she ran the place, but she was a student like the rest of us. She had no right to boss us around just because she had been here longer.

"Well? Are you going to tell us?" I asked.

Pru stepped over the dead raccoon and stopped inches from my face. I could smell her jasmine perfume and bacon breath.

"Well, well, well. Aren't you the curious one, Ms. Lau...zee," she said, making my last name sound like "lousy."

She stood a couple of inches taller and used her height to intimidate me. I wasn't about to cave. As the youngest of four high-achieving brothers and sisters, I'd learned to stand my ground. My two older brothers gave me more than a few knocks on the head for it. My big sister had no shortage of cruel comments to cut me down. But I never let any of them win. I always fought back.

My strict Chinese parents scolded me, saying I should respect my older siblings, but I refused. *Maybe Mom and Dad were tired of me fighting everyone, and that's why they sent me here.*

Pru reminded me of my sister, Agnes. They both thought they knew better than anyone else.

"You were going to tell us who the ghoul is," I said. "I was just trying to spare ourselves the drama."

Her nostrils flared briefly before she forced a fake smile and stepped back. "The ghoul is another victim of the evil force. We now call her the ghoul, but when she was alive her name was Emma Stilton. She was one of the first students who attended classes at Heartwood, back when there were more trees and animals than buildings and students."

She stepped around the dead raccoon, looking down at it as if to build some drama to her story, then continued.

"One day Emma went into these woods against the headmaster's rules. Some say she loved to go for midnight hikes, but I believe she was drawn to the woods. Perhaps by the very force that led Claude Dubois to the top of the tower. What happened to her in the woods, we won't ever know for sure, but it was a horrible end. The next morning Emma was found in very much the same condition as this raccoon."

One of the boys beside me started to gag and covered his mouth. He wore a T-shirt with an imprint of the Hulk's green body on the front, which was a contrast to the boy's scrawny arms. I spotted his name tag—Boston. We all took a step away. Boston didn't puke, but I wasn't taking any chances. I kept my distance. So did everyone else.

"Legend has it the school did not want Emma's death to be a stain on the academy," Pru said. "Instead of reporting it, they lied and said she had run away. They left the body for the ravens to feast on. But death was only the beginning for Emma. Now she is the ghoul who haunts these woods, waiting for the next student to wander too far."

Beside me, a girl with a bob haircut and pink glasses joked, "I guess the ghoul was nearsighted. Couldn't tell a raccoon from a student."

I laughed, as did a few of the other new students. Pru glared and strode up to the girl with the pink glasses. She glanced down at her name tag.

"Ricki, is it?" Pru said. "You think this is funny?"

Ricki smirked. "Not ha-ha funny. More like cringe."

"You break the rules at Heartwood, you'll pay," Pru warned.

"And what are the rules?" I asked.

"I was getting to them!" Pru snapped.

Ricki rolled her hand to signal Pru to hurry up. "Make it fast," she said. "The smell from the *fake* racoon is making me dizzy."

Pru's eyes nearly bulged out of her head. She gritted her teeth and whispered, "That is a real dead raccoon."

I took another look at the dead body. The hole in the animal's chest was perfectly round, and the inside looked more like plastic. Was Ricki right about the body being fake? I started to think this was all a setup. But that changed in a flash. Pru stooped over the raccoon, grabbed a nearby stick, stabbed it into the wound and pulled out a dripping organ.

Boston threw up. Everyone but Ricki jumped back, gasping. A few of the students covered their eyes.

Ricki rubbed Boston's back as she whispered, "It's okay. Just don't look at it."

Pru was enjoying the moment. She held up the stick with the dripping red organ dangling from the end. "Listen up, freshies. Break the rules here and suffer."

"Are you going to tell us already?" I asked.

"Heartwood Academy might have accepted you as a student, but you still have to pass *the test*," Pru said.

"What test?" Boston asked, wiping his mouth.

"It's our way of making sure you're the right kind of Heartwood student," Pru said.

"I thought the right kind was the one whose parents coughed up enough money to get in," Ricki said.

Pru narrowed her gaze at Ricki but ignored the taunt. Instead she addressed the entire group.

"The sophomores are going to lead you into the woods where you have to stay one night. If you last, you're officially in."

"Aren't we already in?" I asked.

Pru smiled. "Not until we seniors say you're in." Then she let out a laugh. I shifted uncomfortably. Her cackle was like the screech of a microphone too close to the speakers.

"What happens if we don't last the night?" Boston asked.

Pru raised the raccoon's heart and smiled. "You don't want to find out."

Chapter Three

Our tour came to an end at the student dorms, a few hundred yards to the left of the school and butted up against another section of the forest. Finally I'd get to see where I'd be sleeping! More ivy crawled all over the side of the stone building. I counted three floors and noted the statues of hunched-over demons perched on the ledge of the top floor, watching us as we climbed the stone steps to the archway entrance. Definite horror-movie vibe.

Our suitcases awaited us at the foot of a wide staircase. The black-and-white tiled floor and pea-green paint on the walls made me wonder, Is this place a dorm or a hospital? On one side of the staircase, images of Heartwood Academy played in a loop on a TV monitor—buildings, staff, teachers and students. On the other side the couple in a large painting gazed down at us.

"Who are they?" Ricki asked.

Pru sniffed. "Claude and Margaret Dubois."

She led us up the staircase. I glanced at the label under the painting. *Three Hearts Forever.*

I grabbed the oak banister with one hand and hauled my heavy bag up the steps. I wasn't the only freshie dragging their luggage up the stairs. We were a symphony of suitcases and grunts.

When we reached the second floor, I noticed the older students lurking in the hallway, smirking at us. No one wore the school uniforms here. Instead T-shirts and jeans were the dorm fashion.

A tall, brown-skinned boy cracked a grin at us.

"Welcome to the zoo," he said.

Pru scowled. "Ignore Jamal."

"Anyone need a hand with their bags?" he asked.

Pru checked the time on her watch—a bright-purple band that matched her purple fingernail polish. "The climb builds character. Let's go, freshies."

There were groans as my fellow freshies heaved their bags up the next flight of stairs. I glanced back at Jamal. He rolled his eyes and imitated Pru's stance, checking an invisible watch on his wrist. Part of me wished he had been the one giving the tour.

When we reached the third floor, Pru pointed down the hallway. Several room doors were wide open.

"The office assigned your rooms. Get to know your roommate, but know that you have exactly one week to change room assignments. The office is generally good with changes in the first week, but after that you're stuck with each other."

I checked my room-assignment sheet and headed to room 312. Ricki rolled her red suitcase toward the same door. She smiled at me. "Three twelve?"

I nodded. "I'm Allie Lau."

"Nice to meet you, Allie. I'm Ricki Mendez. After you."

"Thanks," I said, rolling my black suitcase into the room.

The space was identical on either side. A bed was pushed against the wall. Next to it sat a desk and chair by the one window. And at the foot of each bed was a closet.

"You want the left or the right?" I asked Ricki.

"If you don't mind, I'll take the right," she said. "More sun for my aloe plant."

I kicked my heavy suitcase to the left side of the room and unpacked my clothes. After a couple of hours, our dorm room began to show some character. Ricki placed plants on her desk while I pinned a giant poster of my tuxedo cat, Buddy, over my bed. My parents had had the poster printed for me. It was a cruel reminder of the nice things I could no longer have now that I was at Heartwood. I wondered how much trouble I'd have to cause to get kicked out and sent back home.

I peered out the window. Our room faced the forest. I could see the area where we had found the dead raccoon.

"What do you think the dead raccoon was all about?" I asked.

Ricki rolled her eyes. "The test. It's a cringe initiation the seniors make freshies go through every year."

"How do you know?"

"My brother," Ricki said. "Emil went here four years ago, and they put him through the same thing."

"Is that how you knew the raccoon was fake?" I asked.

She nodded. "Yeah. He said that thing's probably as old as the school. But the organ out of the chest was something new. Anyway, we're going to get more of it when we spend the night in the forest, I'm guessing."

"I knew I'd hate this place," I said. "Why don't the teachers or staff do something about it?"

Ricki shrugged. "Don't know."

Knock, knock.

The door was already open. Jamal leaned against the doorframe, grinning at us. "Actually, the school won't do anything because no one wants to kick out a kid who might be related to a major donor. Hey, I love the cat." He nodded at my poster. "Reminds me of my kitty."

"Thanks," I said.

"So I heard you have the inside scoop about the test," Jamal said.

Ricki and I shared a quick look. *What was he going to do?*

"Relax," he said. "I hate it too. When I was a freshie, they had us out on a miserable night. Cold. Rainy. But the senior in charge wouldn't stop it. Half of us were sick with colds after."

Ricki crossed her arms. "Why don't you stop it then?"

"Not my call," Jamal said. "I'm a sophomore. It's just my second year here. Pru's the top dog, and she calls the shots."

"Plus you probably want to dish out some of the crap you got," I said.

He shook his head. "Nah. I hated the test when I was a freshie. Still do."

"But you'll let us suffer," I said.

"Don't have a choice," he said. "Pru wouldn't think twice about making me do the test over again."

Ricki sighed. "Can't be as bad as what my brother went through. The seniors dumped worms on his head while he was hiding in a hole. Emil can't even look at a bowl of ramen without freaking out."

"You're going to get it worse," Jamal said. "Pru's brother was the one in charge when I did the test, and Pru's, like, a thousand times worse than he was."

I stiffened.

He stepped into the room. "If you want to avoid the worst of it, I can tell you where to hang out."

Ricki narrowed her gaze. "Why would you want to help us? You don't owe us anything."

Jamal threw up his hands. "Easy, there. I come in peace. During the test, I started to have a panic attack. Pru's brother thought I was faking it, but one of the sophomores helped me. Found me a spot in the forest where I could ride out the night without getting hassled. I figured I'd pay it forward."

"Why us?" I asked.

He looked over his shoulder before speaking. "Whatever you two did during the tour has pissed

Pru off. She's been talking about you two for the last hour. She's decided to teach you a lesson. I figure anyone who can get under her skin might need my help."

Ricki smiled. "Well...thanks."

"But you two have to do one thing for me," he said.

"What?" I asked.

"Pretend to take the test seriously," Jamal said.

"Why?" Ricki asked.

He glanced into the hallway and closed the door. "If Pru's anything like her brother, this test is going be cruel. Right now she's headed to the cafeteria with buckets. I heard her say something about looking for meat scraps and pig's blood."

"Shouldn't you report her?" Ricki asked.

Jamal shook his head. "Told you. No one wants to mess with a donor kid. And if she finds out, she'll get her buddies to make my life miserable for the rest of the year."

"She sounds nice," Ricki snarked, rolling her eyes.

"Hey, if Pru sees that the stunts aren't working on you, she'll ramp everything up to eleven. And you definitely don't want that."

"Okay," I said.

"And whatever you do, please don't let on that I'm helping you. If Pru finds out, I'm dead. Okay?"

I glanced at Ricki. She nodded. I offered my hand to Jamal.

"Deal," I said.

He shook my hand, then Ricki's.

"When the test night comes, I'll be your guide," Jamal said. "I'll take you where you won't be bothered too much."

"When is the test?" I asked.

"Most likely the first Saturday. That's when most of the staff are gone. Just a couple of cook staff left. Pru will have the run of the place for the weekend." He opened the door. "Remember, don't let on."

He left, closing the door behind him. I walked to the window and stared at the forest beyond the school grounds.

"Ricki, do you think Pru will come up with something worse than the raccoon?" I asked.

She walked up beside me. "I think we can count on it."

I chewed my bottom lip and hoped Jamal would hold up his end of the bargain.

Chapter Four

For the rest of the week I slogged through my new routine. Go to class. Eat bland cafeteria food. Do my homework. Talk with other freshies about the test. Try to fall asleep beside my very noisy roommate. Turned out Ricki was not only a snorer but also a sleep talker. Well, more like a sleep screamer.

As I tossed and turned in bed the first night, I tried to piece together Ricki's strange talking dream.

"Keep your claws off my face! Don't eat the parrot. Ahhh, I'm trapped. The ice! It burns! It tickles.

I'm gone!" she moaned, looking more like a body in a coffin than a girl dreaming.

I buried my head under my pillow to muffle her one-sided conversation. On the third night, I even considered putting the pillow over *her* face to silence her screams for good. It left me feeling grumpy and groggy every day. Thank goodness for the coffee vending machine in the cafeteria.

By the end of the week, all I wanted to do was bury myself under my comforter and get some peace and quiet. When Friday came I expected to get a good night's sleep before the test on Saturday. But Pru and fate had other plans. She gathered all the older students and freshies in the rec area just before supper. She had ditched her green jacket and skirt and replaced it with a black turtleneck sweater and jeans.

"Freshies, eat well tonight," Pru said. "Because after dinner, you'll need all your strength for the test."

Tonight? Jamal had said it was going to happen

on Saturday. Had he lied to us? Was this a setup? I glanced in his direction. He looked as surprised as I felt. The older seniors gathered behind Pru and leered at us.

I glanced at the nervous freshies around the room. If fear had a look, it would be a picture of all these wide-eyed kids. If fear had a smell, it would be the stench of their stress BO. I jumped back when I realized I was right next to Boston. I hoped he wouldn't puke again.

"The rules are simple," Pru said. "Survive the night in the forest and hope that the ghoul doesn't find you. Return to the dorm before the sun rises? You fail the test. Call for help on your phone? That's a fail. Disobey your senior? Fail."

Boston raised his hand. "What happens if we don't pass the test?"

The seniors laughed. A few rubbed their hands gleefully. Pru cracked an evil grin. "What's your name again?"

"Boston," he replied. "Like the band, not the cream pie. My grandpa was a roadie for them."

"You ever hear of do-overs, Boston?" Pru asked.

He slowly nodded.

"No one ever fails the test," Pru said. "They just do it over and over until they get it right. Oh, and one new rule I've added for this year. If one of you fails tonight, you all will have to take the test again next weekend."

"That's not fair," Ricki blurted. "My brother never had to do that."

Pru grinned. "Yes, I heard some of you have family who attended Heartwood Academy before. I figured they might have warned you about the test, so I decided to add a few twists. Anyone mind?"

The seniors laughed. Most of the sophomores chuckled. A couple flashed us looks of pity.

I raised a hand. "This isn't fair," I said. "Not everyone had a brother or sister who came here before. Why do we all have to suffer because of it?"

Pru smiled at me. “Simple, *Lousy*. Seniors make the rules.”

I was about to speak up, but I spotted Jamal shaking his head. Not enough for anyone else to notice. But it was a definite signal to shut up. I remembered our deal. I had to go along if he was going to find a safe place for Ricki and me.

“Sorry,” I mumbled. “I’m not good with being outdoors.”

She nodded. “Good girl. After dinner meet in the dorm lobby, and we’ll get things started.”

I gritted my teeth as I surveyed the faces of the senior students. They all looked eager to run us through the test. I wasn’t about to give Pru the satisfaction of her winning. I wondered how tough the other freshies were. Would one of them phone for help and force the rest of us to suffer a second night in the woods? No way was I going to let this go on.

I skipped dinner and ducked out of the cafeteria. I headed to the main building and sprinted up to the third floor. Someone on the staff would have to do something about Pru. The staff area was quiet, most of the teachers already gone for the weekend. I marched into the main office where Ms. Benton, the receptionist, was clearing the paperwork. She glanced up when the door opened.

"Ms. Lau, is something wrong?" she asked.

"I'd like to talk to the headmaster," I said.

She rolled down the sleeves of her beige blouse. "I'm afraid you're too late. Mr. Holmes left hours ago. Maybe I can be of assistance."

"It's about Pru Cotton," I said. "She's going to haze the new students tonight. I heard she's going to torture us."

Ms. Benton straightened her black-rimmed glasses. "It's going to be all right, Ms. Lau. Have a seat."

"I'm okay standing," I said. "Don't you believe me?"

She leaned against the edge of the oak desk. "Of course I do. At Heartwood we want our students to be able to solve issues on their own. If you have a problem with Ms. Cotton, we want to give you the opportunity to work it out yourself. Have you talked to her about your concerns?"

"No, but I heard she's going to get blood from the kitchen and cover us with it," I said. "That's not a problem. That's abuse."

She buttoned one of the cuffs of her blouse. "Mr. Holmes has set strict guidelines about the test. No physical contact, either direct or indirect. If Ms. Cotton crosses the line, she'll be punished. Do you have proof that she's going to do this?"

I paused. "It's what I heard."

"Well, Ms. Lau, the kitchen staff would have reported if a student requested blood. So far, I have not heard a thing about blood requests."

"Pru might be getting it on her own," I said.

Ms. Benton sighed. "Look, there just isn't enough time for us to investigate everything a student has heard. That's why Heartwood stresses the importance of students working things out before they come to us. This is how Heartwood builds the world's future leaders. Do you understand?"

I wanted to say, *Yes, you're too chicken to tick off a donor kid.* Instead I nodded. The staff was going to be of no help. I headed back to the dorm.

As I walked along the cobblestone path, I thought about the test. Was Jamal going to help us? I had to believe he would. Maybe I could also convince him to help the other freshies. If we could make it through the one night, we could all put this nonsense behind us.

After dinner, Pru, the sophomores and the freshies gathered at the base of the dorm staircase. I stood under the watchful eyes of the Dubois, watching as sophomores picked their freshies for the test. Each one chose two freshies. Hold on, I thought. *Where were the seniors?* I gave Ricki a WTF shrug. Did she also notice the missing students?

She leaned over and whispered, "They're probably in the forest, waiting for us."

That made sense. I wondered how many kids were lurking in the woods. How many cheap jump scares could they spring on the new kids? I didn't care. I had no plans to be the next victim. I only needed to know where to hide for the night. Jamal was the last sophomore in the room. He flashed a quick smile at me as he headed toward Ricki and me.

"Hold on, Jamal," Pru said.

He stopped smiling and turned around. "What's up?"

She pointed at the other remaining freshies—Boston and the mousy girl, Kayla. "You take them."

He paused. "I can take all four of them, Pru."

"No," she said. "I'll take Ricki and Lousy."

Jamal didn't budge.

"You deaf? Take them," she barked. "Now."

Jamal shook himself out of his daze and pointed at Boston and Kayla. "You two. With me. March."

They headed out, leaving Ricki and me as the last pair standing.

Pru beamed at us. "You two really like raising trouble, don't you?"

I said nothing. Ricki followed suit.

"I'm going to enjoy this," Pru said. "We're going to have so much *fun*."

The way she stressed *fun* gave me shivers. This was going to be a long night.

Chapter Five

A chilly wind bit into my face as I walked toward the forest. Clouds had drifted across the full moon, leaving only the lamps along the school path to light the way. As we left the dorm, I thought at first that Pru was going to take us into the school. But she strayed from the cobblestone path leading to the L-shaped building, cut across the dewy grass and strode toward the edge of the woods. My heart beat fast as I focused on the glow from Pru's lantern. Ricki and I entered the woods after her, and the forest swallowed the little light coming from the school grounds. The test had begun.

Pru raised her lantern to light a narrow trail between the trees. Ricki fell in behind me as I followed our guide.

Suddenly a scream rang out from somewhere deep in the forest.

Pru spun around. “I think the ghoul is here.”

Ricki shivered. “I should have brought a sweater. How deep into the woods do we have to go? I think maybe we should go back now.”

“Ready to give up already?” Pru asked.

Ricki slowly shook her head. “No. Not yet. I guess.”

Pru smiled, then lowered her lantern and walked ahead.

I nudged Ricki. “Are you scared?” I whispered.

“No, but we have to put on a good show or else Pru will make it worse,” she said. “I overheard Jamal talking to a couple of the sophomores in the cafeteria yesterday. Even they agreed that Pru was taking things too far."

"What did they say?" I asked.

Ricki leaned closer. "They were talking about leading us to a part of the forest that is off-limits to everyone. Said that's where a hermit has a camp."

"What's that?"

"It's someone who has decided to cut out the world and just live off the land," Ricki explained. "They said he might be like an ex-convict or something. And he's protective of his camp and is armed. No one wanted to be on the team going near his camp, but it sounded like Pru wanted to go through with it."

"Can she get away with it?" I asked. "We should tell the dorm monitors."

"She's the head monitor," Ricki said. "They all have to listen to her."

I chewed my bottom lip, thinking. It was bad enough having to deal with Pru's cruel seniors, but the idea of a hermit who might attack us did not sit well with me. I wondered if we could catch up to Jamal and get him to lead us away from the guy. If the older kids were afraid of this guy, I was sure Jamal would do anything to stay away from his camp, even disobey Pru's orders.

I scanned the woods, searching for him and his freshies. Jamal's group had left a few minutes before us, so it made sense that the closest light would come from his lantern. The woods were dark. I wondered if the other sophomores had steered clear of the hermit's camp and Pru had ignored all the warnings because she wanted us to meet him. I shuddered, but not from the cold.

Ricki began to wheeze. She reached into her pocket and pulled out an inhaler. She shook it a few times before she took a puff. She muttered, "Nuts."

"You okay?" I asked.

She nodded. "My inhaler's almost out. I should be fine as long as I don't have to run."

I lowered my voice. "Do you have another? When we find Jamal, maybe he can run back and get it. Keep your eyes peeled for him."

Ricki pocketed her inhaler. "I'll be fine. Really."

"You sure? We can go back," I said.

She waved me off. "I'm not making everyone do the test again. Go on. I'll catch up."

I patted Ricki on the arm, then pushed ahead toward Pru's lantern light. I needed a plan B in case we couldn't find Jamal. That meant sucking up to Pru. Definitely not in my nature, but for Ricki's sake, I had to ignore the part of my brain that said, "Fight." I glanced back at Ricki to make sure she was okay. She waved me to go on. I nodded and caught up to Pru. She turned as she heard my approach and lifted her lantern.

A howl echoed through the trees, followed by several frightened screams. I noticed Pru staring at me, watching for a reaction. *Ah!* I'd pieced together the prank. Her lifting the lantern and the screams seemed to be connected. That was how she signaled the seniors hiding in the woods. I couldn't let on that I knew. Instead I jumped and shrieked, playing the part of a frightened freshie.

"Pru, Pru," I said, panting. "Did you hear that?"

She smiled. "Yes, the ghoul's not happy about something."

"I don't like this at all," I whined.

She aimed the lantern at my face. "We're only getting started, Lousy."

I paused and sucked in my breath, pretending to summon my courage. "What else can happen?"

She grinned. "You'll see."

She turned and continued through the woods. I kept up the act as we trudged through the forest. Pru walked faster, and I nearly tripped on some tree roots as I stumbled after her.

"Can I use my phone?" I asked. "It'd be easier for me to find my way. You don't want us to get separated, do you?"

"Use your phone and fail," she said.

"But you said we'd fail if we used our phones to call for help," I pointed out. "You didn't say anything about using our phones as lights."

She said nothing but slowed down, allowing me to keep pace with her. I looked up at the night sky. The clouds still blocked out the moon. Around us the dark trees stood at attention, hiding any seniors waiting to jump out at me.

"Hey, Pru," I said. "That story about the ghoul. It's all made up, right?"

She leaned forward. "Do you believe in ghosts?"

"No. Yes. Maybe," I said, pretending to sound scared. "Do you?"

"There are plenty of things that happen in this forest that I can't explain," Pru said. "None of the staff can explain it either. So I keep an open mind to any possibilities."

"Including ghosts," I said.

"Especially that."

She lifted her lantern. Almost as if on cue, a scream erupted from the woods. It sounded closer this time. I grabbed her arm, pretending I hadn't expected the scream.

"The ghoul's getting closer," Pru hissed. "I think she knows we're here."

"We should run," I said.

Pru stood her ground, refusing to budge. "She'll find you no matter what you do."

A girl screamed, but she was cut off by a fit of coughing. This caught Pru off guard. Her lantern was down by her side. Her expression twisted into a question mark as she scanned the dark woods around us.

"What's the matter?" I asked.

"Where's the other freshie?" she asked.

I looked back. Ricki was gone.

Chapter Six

"Ricki!" I shouted.

"Freshie! Where are you?" Pru called.

The woods were silent. No sign of my roommate.

"Ricki!" I screamed.

Silence. Was this part of the test? Or had we trespassed on the hermit's campsite?

Pru grabbed my arm. "You two dickheads are ruining the test. Tell your friend to stop messing around and come out."

I pulled away. "Let go."

She pushed me away and ran into the woods. "Freshie!" she called out, lifting her lamp.

Ah, another signal. When Pru lifted her lamp, the seniors would do something to creep me out. I waited for a scream or howl. I spun around, half expecting one of them to lunge at me from behind. Nothing.

"Freshie! Get back here right now, or I swear you will regret it!" Pru spun in all directions as she spouted her threat. "You have ten seconds to show your face!"

"What are you up to?" I asked.

She didn't answer. She just kept crashing through the trees and calling for Ricki. I began to doubt if this was part of the test. Maybe Ricki had come across the hermit.

I yelled to Pru, "The last place I saw her was over here!" I waved for her to follow me. She did.

I was worried about Ricki's asthma and her inhaler running out. What if she'd had an attack and couldn't breathe? I kicked myself for not slowing down for her.

"Ricki!" Pru screamed. "Come out now!"

We ran deeper into the forest. Pru got ahead of me. I tried to keep up, but I slammed into a fallen log. Pru kept running, leaving me in the dark. I couldn't keep pace without crashing into a tree or tripping on a root.

Screw the rules! I pulled my phone from my back pocket and tapped on the flashlight. I scanned the forest floor. If Ricki had had an attack and collapsed, she'd most likely be lying on the ground. I moved to the right, pushing through deep brush. I kept moving through the woods, pushing my toe ahead, hoping to make contact with Ricki.

Then I noticed the edge of something solid jutting from the bushes. Odd. It was smooth and straight. Not a branch or a bush. I inched closer. It was the top of a stone that stood about knee height. I would have walked past it if I weren't looking down for Ricki's body. I stooped and cleared the bush out of the way. A name and dates were etched into the front of the stone marker.

Claude Dubois

April 13, 1793–December 12, 1835

A gravestone! Shocked, I stumbled back. My leg slammed into another stone. *Crack!* I aimed my phone at what I had run into. Another gravestone. I was in the middle of a damn cemetery. Fear had shot through my entire body at the first discovery, and I was fighting hard now to slow my breathing and calm my heart. I tried to convince myself that this was part of the test. The gravestones looked like they had been here for a long time. And one of them just happened to belong to Heartwood's founder. This had to be a setup.

Screw it. No way was I going to give Pru the satisfaction. I kicked at the second gravestone, knocking off a large chunk. I kept kicking until the whole stone toppled to the ground. *Thud.*

I started to kick Claude's gravestone. *Ouch. Bad idea.* This one was solid. I limped away, stepping over the other stone and looking for Pru. Her lantern beam bobbed in the woods ahead of me. I walked off the pain in my foot as I caught up to Pru.

I thumbed off my phone light before she could see me. I shouted, "Pru! Pru! Did you find Ricki?"

She stopped and raised her lantern, aiming the beam at my face. "No. She's gone," Pru said, her eyes wide with panic.

"You know she needs a new inhaler," I said. "If we don't get her help soon, she could die out here."

"Why do you think I'm calling for her?" she said.

I crossed my arms over my chest. "Then get on your phone and call off the test. The two of us searching in the woods could take forever. If everyone were here, we'd have a better shot at finding Ricki."

She stomped toward me, the lantern beam blinding me. I squinted and noticed the anger flashing in Pru's eyes.

"The nerve of you," she snarled. "I'm the dorm monitor. What I say goes. What makes you think you know better than me?"

"All I know is that the dorm monitor is the one who is going to get the blame if Ricki dies on her watch. Especially if the headmaster learns you took us into an off-limits area."

"I don't know what you're talking about," Pru said, adjusting the purple band of her watch.

"Yeah, right," I said. "We heard about your plans to take us to the hermit. You thought it'd be fun to give us a real scare, but you didn't think about what the guy would do when we trespassed on his camp. If something happens to Ricki, it's on your head."

"*Arrrrooooooooo...*"

We both froze. "What was that?" I whispered.

"I don't know."

I looked around for the source of the sound.

"*Ooooooooughhhh...*"

The moaning seemed to come from the graveyard.

"What the..." Pru muttered, lifting her lantern.

Something was up. The moans continued, followed by a sound like feet dragging.

Pru screamed, "Who's there?!"

"*Oooorrrrrrrrmmmmmmaaaa...*"

I backed up, scanning the woods. Beside me Pru panted. I glanced over and saw her wide-eyed panic. She had played her part to the hilt so far. But was she this good an actor?

"Run!" Pru screamed. She sprinted away from the sound.

I hesitated. My body tingled with nervous energy. My mind was willing my body to stay still. *Great school you sent me to, Mom*. The moaning grew louder. What if it was the hermit? I couldn't stick around to find out.

I bolted away, running toward Pru's lantern beam. The light looked faint in the distance. How could she get that far away so fast? Was my mind playing tricks, or was the dark forest messing with my sense of distance? I set my sights on the fading glow and sprinted toward it.

Suddenly the light blinked out, and I heard a strangled scream. I froze. I was alone and at the mercy of whatever was in the woods.

Chapter Seven

I hated standing in the dark woods with no way to defend myself. If the noise was coming from the hermit, I had no idea what he might do, but I wouldn't go down without a fight. I lowered my stance and prepared to spring out at any attacker. I'd had enough practice scrapping with my brothers to defend myself. I wanted to pull out my phone and turn on the light, but I realized that as soon as I turned it on, the hermit would know my exact location. Right now darkness was my only advantage.

The dragging footsteps got louder.

I wanted to fight but needed a weapon, better light and room to swing. In the middle of all these trees, I was a sitting duck. I had to find an area that gave me space to fight and an exit route if I needed one. I got down on all fours and began to crawl through the forest.

It seemed the guy making the dragging sounds knew where I was going. The footsteps followed me and grew louder. I had to get out of here fast.

I crawled along the ground, stones and pine needles digging into my palms. My knees were damp and dirty from the soil I'd been crawling over. All the while, the footsteps continued after me.

Finally I reached a small clearing. The clouds had drifted past the moon, which now cast a faint glow across the area. I stayed at the edge of the clearing, keeping my back to a large tree. I was glad

I had chosen to wear black for the test. It would be harder for the hermit to spot me. At least, I hoped that was the case.

The dragging footsteps stopped. My plan had worked. The man was confused, unsure where I had gone, which gave me the advantage. Now I needed a weapon.

I felt along the ground for rocks. Nothing was big enough to do any damage, but a few stones were hefty enough to make a distracting noise. If I couldn't fight, maybe I could send the guy on a wild-goose chase.

I couldn't see what I was grabbing. I moved my hand along the damp soil—roots, twigs, pebbles. Then I felt something hard and smooth—a rock about the size of a baseball. I scooped it up and placed it in my lap, then combed the area with both hands, finding another four rocks about the same size. I hoped they'd be enough to send the hermit running in any direction other than where I was.

I lifted up the bottom of my shirt and piled the rocks into the makeshift hammock. Then I stood up and listened. Still no sign of anyone. I grabbed one of the rocks and searched for a target. A fallen log in the middle of the clearing. Perfect. I aimed and tossed. *Thwock!*

I waited for the sound of footsteps, counting silently. One...two...three...four...five...

When I reached twenty, I figured the guy hadn't heard me. I pulled the second rock from my shirt hammock and hurled it hard at the log. It sailed wide. *Damn it.* I pulled out the third rock and carefully aimed before tossing it. *Thwock!*

I leaned against the tree and listened for any sign of life from the woods. Nothing. Then came the sound of dragging footsteps in the distance. *Great.* He had taken the bait. I tossed the fourth rock at the log to make sure he knew to come to the clearing. *Thwock!*

The footsteps quickened, followed by a low moan of pain. The sound came from the other side of the clearing. I quickly slipped behind the tree with my final rock. I would use this to send the hermit running in the opposite direction of where I planned to go. I waited for him to appear in the clearing first. I wanted to know exactly where he was before I ran away.

Another moan, loud and painful. I braced myself, waiting for the hermit to leave the woods. Any minute the guy was going to shamble into the clearing. Any minute.

I held my breath as I saw the brush shaking to my far right. I gripped the last rock, preparing to hurl it as far as possible. A figure emerged from the edge of the clearing. In the eerie moonlight, the figure looked like a ghost. I couldn't quite make out their face, and they looked down as they shambled forward. They moaned as they limped toward the log.

The limping figure stopped and lifted their head. The moon's glow lit up the face and pink glasses. My jaw dropped open. Ricki!

I dropped the rock and stepped out from behind the tree. "Ricki," I hissed.

She staggered toward me, wheezing and gasping. I reached into my pocket, pulled out my phone and thumbed on the flashlight mode.

"Allie," Ricki moaned. "Help me."

The beam lit up her face. Her glasses were sitting at an odd angle. She reached up with her hand, which was covered in blood. Then she collapsed.

Chapter Eight

"Ricki!" I screamed, springing from my hiding place behind the tree and rushing into the moonlit clearing.

Her body was face down. I nearly tripped on a tree root but avoided face-planting beside my roommate. I knelt at her side. Should I roll her over or shake her awake? What was I supposed to do here? Calm down, I told myself. I shone the light across Ricki's body. I couldn't tell if she was breathing.

I touched her back. “Ricki?”

No answer.

I grabbed her shoulder and gently shook her. “Can you hear me?”

Still nothing.

Do I call for help? Not yet. I pocketed the phone and rolled Ricki over on her back.

A stream of blood trickled out the side of her mouth, and her eyes were wide open.

“Ricki!” I screamed.

No reaction. I reached for my phone. But just as I began to call, laughter filled the air, coming from the edge of the clearing. I lowered my phone and looked around. Jamal and a muscle-bound sophomore emerged from the trees, along with four freshies. The freshies looked like they had been through the wringer.

“Sorry,” Ricki said.

I turned my attention back to my roommate.

"You okay?" I asked.

She sighed. "Not exactly. I'm still wheezing." She propped herself up on her elbows and spit the blood out of her mouth. "Hate the taste of fake blood," she complained as she sat up and wiped the red stuff from her lips and chin.

"Wait! You're in on this? I don't understand," I said.

The lantern snapped on and lit up the clearing. Everyone jogged over. Anger rose to the back of my throat, and I wanted to spit venom at Jamal. Had he set us up all along?

"Why did you do it?" I asked Ricki.

"I had no choice, Allie." She reached for my hand, but I pulled away. "They said if I did this I could go back to the dorm and get my new inhaler without failing the test."

Jamal stopped a few feet away from me. "Well, it looks like we have two more freshies who passed the test."

I glared at him. He chuckled. "The look on your face when you saw Ricki was priceless. I wish we had filmed it, eh, Colin?"

Colin mocked me. "*Rickiiiiiiiiiii!*"

The freshies looked down at their feet.

"It's funny, freshies," Colin snarled. "Laugh!"

The freshies reluctantly chuckled along.

"Chill, Colin. That's enough," Jamal said as he reached a hand to help me up.

I waved it off. "I don't want your help."

He mouthed, *Sorry*.

I climbed to my feet along with Ricki. "You're all sick. All of you. What if the hermit had gotten Ricki or me?"

This sparked more laughter from Colin. The freshies stared at the ground.

Colin caught his breath and pointed at Ricki. "She fell for it. I can't believe these freshies fell for it."

Ricki glared at him. "What are you talking about?"

Colin explained, "Pru figured you two weren't keen on the ghoul story, so she came up with a new one to give you something to really freak out about. And you bought it all! Losers."

Jamal waved him off. "Okay, these two passed the test. We can send them back to the dorm to get her inhaler. Pru, that okay with you? Pru?"

No answer. He looked around the edge of the clearing.

"Where's Pru?" Colin asked.

I shrugged. "Don't know. Don't care."

Ricki said, "I have no idea. I hadn't seen her since Jamal grabbed me in the woods and you jerks made me put the fake-blood capsule in my mouth."

"Anyone see Pru?" Jamal asked.

Everyone shook their heads.

"Pru's lantern blinked out when I heard a scream... Oh wait, is this another part of the test?" I asked. "Because I think we've all had enough of this."

Several of the freshies nodded in agreement.

Jamal and Colin separated and headed off to different parts of the forest. "Pru! Pru!" Their lantern beams lit up the woods, but there was no sign of her.

I sighed. "Okay, this isn't funny anymore!" I yelled after them. "You can cut out the act!"

Jamal ignored me. "Pru! Come out. It's done. They passed!"

Ricki elbowed me. "You'd figure she'd want a front-row seat, after the way we made fun of her."

I nodded. "Yeah. I mean, she wanted to lead us out here. Why wouldn't she want to see us suffer?"

Jamal and Colin came running back to the clearing. "Where was the last place you saw Pru?" Colin demanded. I could see beads of sweat on his forehead. This wasn't part of the test.

"I don't know. Over there somewhere, I think." I pointed in the direction of the path I'd taken. "It was near the gravestones you put up."

Jamal raised an eyebrow. "What gravestones?"

"Don't play innocent," I said. "The two stones in the woods over there."

"What are you talking about?" Jamal asked.

"Never mind her," Colin said. "Text Pru."

"Good idea," Jamal said. He pulled his phone out of his pocket. He tapped on the screen and waited for a response. After a few minutes he texted again. Nothing.

Jamal shook his head. "She's not answering. Where is Pru?"

Chapter Nine

Jamal elbowed Colin. "Text the others. See if Pru is with them."

The mood had shifted. Colin wasn't laughing anymore, and the freshies nervously looked at one another.

"No one's replying," Colin said.

Jamal ran his hand through his hair. "Try calling them."

Colin shook his head. "We call them, their ringers will warn the other freshies where they are."

Jamal cut in. "The test doesn't matter anymore. If Pru is hurt or lost, we're all going to be in trouble. You know who her parents are?"

Colin stiffened.

"Who?" Ricki asked.

"They're Heartwood Academy's biggest donors," Jamal said. "And they are not going to be okay with us losing their only daughter. We have to find her now. Call the others!"

Colin held up his phone and punched in the number. I inched closer to Ricki. "Do you think this is a part of the test?"

She pursed her lips. "I'm not sure. Jamal and Colin look pretty panicked."

"Why aren't you answering?" Colin shouted at his phone.

"Maybe she's in a dead zone," I suggested.

Colin sniffed at me, dismissing my idea.

Jamal shook his head. "No, man. I think she's right. Where's Robbie? She headed off before me.

She's got to be the closest to us."

Colin pointed to the right. "She was down by the river."

"Okay, go look for her," Jamal ordered. "The rest of you freshies go back to the dorm and get help."

Colin grabbed Jamal's arm. "Hold on. We'll get in trouble if they tell the staff what happened."

Jamal scowled. "That's what you care about right now?"

"Yeah," Colin said. "My dad said I get one more strike and then he's yanking me out and sending me to the local school. They don't even have a workout room."

"Not my problem," Jamal said. "We have to find Pru now."

Colin jabbed an accusing finger at me. "She's the one who was with her last. What did you do to Pru?"

I backed up and bumped into Ricki. "I don't know. This is your twisted game."

"Allie's right," Ricki said. "You toads are the ones running this test. You should know where your leader is."

Colin got so close to my face that I could smell the garlic and ketchup he'd had for dinner. I winced.

Jamal grabbed Colin and yanked him back. "That's enough."

"What? Why? You crushing on the little freshie?" Colin snapped.

"Shut it," Jamal ordered, stepping up and using his height to get Colin to back down. Jamal turned to the freshies. "What are you waiting for? Go!"

The freshies scrambled into the woods.

"Go with them," Jamal barked at Ricki and me.

Colin shoved Jamal. "Screw you. I'm not taking the fall for Pru going missing."

The two boys faced off against each other, both refusing to back down. Ricki grabbed my arm.

"I think we should go with the others."

I nodded and began to follow Ricki.

"*Unnnnmmmmggggggghhhhh!!*"

"What was that?" I asked.

"Where's it coming from?" Ricki asked.

I listened, trying to pinpoint the source of the moaning.

"I think it's coming from over there," Ricki said, nodding to the area where I had been hiding.

The two boys stopped arguing and turned toward the sound. Colin began to walk toward the edge of the clearing. Jamal raised his lantern to light the area. Ricki and I inched forward to get a closer view.

"*Ummnnnnnnngggghhhh!*"

This has to be another part of the test, I told myself. But one doubt nagged at the back of my head. If the goal was to freak out the freshies, why was Pru targeting her own sophomores? Maybe Pru found out about Jamal offering to help us. Was this her way of putting him in his place?

Colin raised his phone and turned on the light as he approached the trees. The moaning grew louder. As hard as I tried to convince myself this was another part of the test, my rapidly beating heart did not believe it.

Ricki gasped, "What is that?"

A man, or what used to be a man, shuffled from the trees. He wore a black suit with long tails, but the jacket was frayed and soiled. It looked more like rags hanging from a rail-thin body. The man's face seemed almost skeletal, with sunken eyes, strangled tufts of beard and loose skin that nearly sagged off his cheeks.

"I thought the story about the hermit was a setup," I said.

"It was. I don't know who that is," Jamal said.

Colin stepped back, covering his mouth and nose. "Oh man, this guy reeks. He smells like rotting meat."

Even from where we stood, I could smell the man.

Colin flexed his biceps and snarled, "Back off, dude. I mean it."

"Run!" I yelled.

Suddenly the man grabbed Colin by the throat and lifted him up.

"Let go of him!" Jamal shouted, rushing at the two.

But before Jamal could even take two steps, the rotting man hurled Colin across the clearing. The beefy boy fell to the ground like a rag doll. Ricki sprinted over to check on him. I stared at the rotting man. Where had he come from? Who was he? Was this another setup?

The man stabbed a bony finger at me.

"Yuuuuuuuuuuuuu..."

Jamal grabbed my hand and pulled me away. "Run!" he barked.

Instinct kicked in, and I ran. "Ricki!" I screamed. "Go!"

She was kneeling beside Colin, trying to wake him up. The rotting man growled at them, then turned his attention to me. His black eyes fixed on me as he opened his mouth. Worms crawled out. I nearly gagged at the sight. The rotting man had set his sights on me. I left Ricki and ran for my life.

Chapter Ten

Branches slapped my face as I chased after Jamal. He kept a steady pace but looked back and slowed down to allow me to catch up. I could hear the rotting man even over my heavy breathing. His moans cut into my ears like nails on a chalkboard.

My lungs burned as I zigged and zagged between the trees. Jamal pushed a heavy branch out of the way, but it slipped out of his grip and swung right at me, catching me on the side and spinning me around. I nearly lost my phone, but I managed to hang on to it. I aimed the light back at the rotting man.

The creep was still limping toward us. Nothing slowed him down. He pushed against a small tree. *Crack!* The tree began to topple over. Who was this guy?

I sprinted up a hill. Jamal reached out and took my hand to pull me to the top.

"Tell me this is part of the test," I panted.

Jamal aimed the lantern beam at the rotting man. "You saw how far he threw Colin. You think any kid can do that? No way. That is next-level."

"He looks like a zombie," I said.

"Are you serious? Like in *The Walking Dead*?"

"I didn't say it was one. I said it looked like one."

"*Umnnggggghhh...*"

"Sounds like one too," I added.

"I don't want to stick around to find out if it is one," Jamal said. "Let's go!"

He grabbed my hand and pulled me away. We dashed through the forest, trying to outrun the rotting man. We crashed through the brush, which cut into my bare arms and face. I wished we could get to an open stretch of field.

The clouds drifted in front of the moon again, leaving the forest dark except for the lantern and my phone light. As I ran, a desperate plan formed in my mind.

"Hold on, Jamal," I said. "Wait."

He stopped.

"Allie, it's not safe here. I can still hear him coming," Jamal said.

"I think I know where the guy came from."

"Who cares? I just want to get away from him."

I grabbed Jamal's shirt.

"Listen to me," I said. "Are you sure Pru didn't set up any gravestones for the test?"

He nodded. "Yeah. I was on the team that set

up the scare sights. No grave markers. It didn't fit Pru's story about the hermit."

"Then if you didn't plant the gravestones, I think that...that...*thing* crawled out of the grave," I explained.

"Are you hearing what you're saying?" Jamal asked.

"Pru talked about an evil force at Heartwood Academy. Something that drove Claude Dubois to jump off the tower. Was that all a setup for this? Or is it a real legend?"

"Oh, crap. He's getting closer," Jamal warned. "We have to go."

He ran ahead of me, clearing a path. I tried to keep up the pace.

"The story of the Dubois family," I said. "Did Pru make it up? Was Margaret talking to spirits?"

"The Heartwood legend is true," Jamal said. "Claude Dubois jumped off the tower. I know that much, but I didn't hear anything about spirits or evil forces."

"But Claude did jump. So that part of the story's real."

Jamal slowed down and looked back. We had outrun the rotting man. For now we were safe.

"As real as anything like that can be," he said, bending over and resting his hands on his knees as he tried to catch his breath.

"Do you believe in ghosts? That maybe Claude's spirit is still here?" I asked.

Jamal tilted his head to one side and narrowed his gaze. "No offense, Allie, but this is sounding like one of Pru's made-up stories. What does Claude Dubois have to do with any of this?"

"The gravestone I saw. It was Claude's grave."

"What? Are you serious?"

"I saw it etched in the marker. I swear, it was Claude Dubois's grave."

"This isn't some bad horror movie," Jamal said.

I looked over my shoulder. No sign of anyone. "I'm having trouble believing it myself, but if this isn't part of the test, then it has to be something. Why not Claude?"

"How about a killer who's buried his victims in the woods and is looking to add to his collection? That would make more sense than the ghost of Claude Dubois."

"Let's find his grave. If it's dug open, we'll know I'm right," I said.

"No way. We're going to find our way back to the school and tell the staff what's going on. No more arguments."

The way Jamal put his foot down reminded me of my parents sending me to Heartwood. *No more arguments.* If I had stood my ground, I wouldn't be in this mess right now. I wasn't about to back down again.

"You do what you want, Jamal," I said. "I'm looking for the grave."

"We have to keep moving," he said. "It's not safe here."

"If the rotting man is Claude, I don't think anywhere is safe right now," I said. "Come with me to find the grave. It's east of the clearing."

Jamal's eyes widened. "East? You're sure?"

"I'm good with directions." I shrugged. "I saw where the moon rose."

He paused, chewing his bottom lip. Finally he spoke. "Okay, let's go."

His reaction seemed odd. He knew more than he was letting on. I led the way, moving quickly through the trees. I stopped after a few feet to listen for Claude. Silence. I continued through the woods.

"So you believe me?" I asked Jamal.

"Not saying I do, but..." He trailed off.

"What is it, Jamal?"

He explained, "It's probably nothing, but last year I was on a study break. Needed to clear my head. I went for a walk in the woods. East of the clearing."

I nodded.

"I hadn't gone too far before I got this creepy feeling. You know that pit you get in your stomach when you see a bad accident about to happen? It was like that, but a hundred times worse. It almost felt like a hunger out there. Like something wanted me."

"Claude?" I asked.

Jamal shook his head. "I don't know, but it creeped me out enough that I headed back to the dorm. I've stayed away from the east side of the forest ever since. The weird thing was, when I turned around I swear I could hear whispering."

"What did you hear?"

"This sounds stupid, but I heard 'three hearts forever,'" he said.

"Like in the painting? What's it mean?"

Jamal answered, "They said that was the last thing Claude wrote before he jumped from the tower. It became our school motto."

I stopped and turned to face Jamal. "Do you think some force drove him to jump?"

Jamal shook his head. "I don't know. But his turning his estate into a school in honor of Margaret? The guy was serious about his wife. He'd do anything for her."

I skidded to a halt.

"Wait. The other gravestone. That must have been Margaret's," I said.

"There are two graves?"

"I'll show you," I said. "Come on."

I sped toward the clearing. I aimed my phone light in front of us while Jamal held up the lantern to cast light to the right and left of us, keeping a watch for the rotting man.

We were almost at the clearing when I heard a voice call out.

"Hold on," I said, putting my hand against Jamal's chest. His shirt was soaking wet from sweat.

"What is it?" he asked.

"Shhh. Listen."

"Over here," a weak voice called.

"That's Pru!" Jamal said. "Pru! Where are you?" He swept the lantern beam left and right, scanning the forest.

"Here," the voice called out. "I'm here."

I grabbed Jamal's arm and pointed to the left. He aimed the lantern beam through the trees. On the ground a pale-faced Pru raised a hand and waved at us. She was alive!

Chapter Eleven

We rushed over to Pru. Jamal dropped his lantern and knelt beside her. I swept my phone light around the woods to make sure the rotting man wasn't nearby. I shone the phone beam at Pru. Her face looked bruised, and blood seeped from a wound on the side of her head. Her blond hair was all matted with it.

Jamal gently helped her sit up.

Pru scanned the woods. "We have to get out. He could be anywhere. We have to go now!"

He put his hands on her shoulders. “What happened?”

“He came out of nowhere. Grabbed me from behind. His hands reeked.” She shuddered. “His face. His hands. The smell.”

“Slow down, Pru,” I said.

“I ran, but he kept coming. I tripped. Rolled down this hill. Couldn’t get up. He was going to kill me. You have to get me out of here.”

Jamal helped Pru to her feet. “We’ll get you back to the dorm.”

“Where is he? Did you see him?” Pru asked, her eyes wide.

“We saw him. But I don’t know where he is,” I said, scanning the woods.

“We have to go *now*!” Pru ordered.

Jamal picked up the lantern and draped one of Pru’s arms around his neck.

“Mind my watch,” she warned, glancing at her purple watch band. “It’s from Ariana’s personal collection. It's worth a fortune."

I rolled my eyes. Even with her life on the line, Pru was more worried about her things.

Jamal wrapped his free hand around her waist. He helped her limp forward. I followed, watching the woods for any sign of her attacker.

"Allie thinks the man who attacked you is a zombie—Claude Dubois," Jamal said. "She thinks she's found his grave."

Pru turned, her gaze narrowing. "Are you serious? A zombie?"

I nodded.

"Bull," Pru said.

"Pru, be honest. You didn't plant any gravestones, did you?" Jamal asked.

Pru glared at him. "No. My mom said the Dubois have a family cemetery on the grounds. She said the school kept it quiet. Only the staff and donors know about it. I'm not going to mess with the school founder's resting place. That's an instant 'three strikes and you're out.'"

"I don't know if it's an entire graveyard," I said, "but I found two gravestones. There might be more, but I'm pretty sure the guy who attacked you came out of one of the graves."

"What's your game?" Pru asked. "Didn't like the way I treated you so you're out to get back at me?"

"I'm serious," I said. "That guy who attacked you is Claude Dubois. Let's find his grave, and I'll prove it."

Jamal shook his head. "Forget it, Allie. Pru's hurt and needs help. After we get her to safety, then we can tell the staff to look for the graves. I'm not going back into the woods."

"We have to find the grave," I argued.

"How is that going to help?" Jamal shot back. "If you're wrong, we'll be trapped in the woods with this guy. If you're right, it's not like we can ask Claude to crawl back into his hole. No, the best thing to do is go to the dorm and get help."

He continued walking with Pru through the woods. I wanted to tell them about the gravestone I'd kicked over and how I thought more zombies might come out of the graves. But the idea sounded too strange even to me. I fell in line behind the two and followed them through the forest.

My phone grew hot, so I switched it to the other hand. The battery was heating up from having the flashlight on for so long. I swept the beam across the trees and listened for Claude Dubois's dragging footsteps.

"This is your fault, Pru," Jamal muttered as he helped her along the trail.

"How would I know a creep was going to show up?" Pru said defensively.

"It's Claude Dubois," I said.

"Ghost stories don't work on me," Pru said. "Save it for when you're in charge of the test."

Jamal grunted. "When the headmaster hears what happened tonight, I think that'll be the end of the test forever. And I'm not complaining."

We took another few steps and then I heard Ricki call out.

"Help! He's here! Help!" she yelled.

Colin's voice joined hers. "Get away from her!"

Jamal and Pru froze. I couldn't let my roommate face Claude alone. "We have to find them," I said.

Pru's eyes went wide with fear. "No way! Get me out of here."

"Allie, it's too dangerous," Jamal warned. "The dorm's not far. We can send help."

"Ricki and Colin need help now!" I said.

Pru grabbed Jamal's arm. "Don't you dare leave me alone. Do you know who my parents are? Do you know what they can do to you if you abandon me?"

"It's okay, Pru," he said. "I'm not going to let anything happen to you."

“Do what you want!” I said, sprinting off alone.

I couldn’t hear Ricki or Colin anymore. Was I too late?

Chapter Twelve

My phone light flickered as I ran through the woods. The battery was dying at the worst time possible. I ran another few feet before the light blinked out for good. I slammed into a tree. *Ow.* I raised my hands and tried to feel my way forward. My knee bumped into something hard. I cursed under my breath. How was I going to get to Ricki and Colin in time?

Suddenly a beam of light lit up the area around me. I turned to find the source, shielding my eyes with one hand.

"Who's there?" I asked.

Jamal's voice called out from behind the glow. "It's me."

The light moved toward me until I saw his face.

"What are you doing here? What about Pru?" I asked.

He shrugged. "Pissing off her donor parents is the least of our worries right now. Let's get Ricki and Colin."

He lifted his lantern and lit a path between the trees. I pocketed my dead phone and then headed to the clearing.

"*Umnnnggggghhhh...*"

When Jamal and I reached the area, I could see Claude shaking a tree, but Ricki and Colin were nowhere in sight.

Jamal grabbed my arm and pointed to the left. "Look."

Colin was on the ground, on all fours. He was conscious, but it looked like he was hurt. Why wasn't

Claude attacking him? What was he doing at the tree?

"Allie!" Ricki called out. Her voice was coming from above.

"Jamal, point the lantern up the tree," I said.

He did. The beam caught Ricki's terrified face as she clung to the tree trunk, about fifteen feet up. Claude couldn't climb, so instead he was rocking the tree, trying to shake Ricki out of it.

She was having trouble keeping her grip. "Ahhhh! I can't hang on!"

Jamal tossed me the lantern and charged at Claude.

"Careful!" I shouted as I fumbled with the lantern. I held it up to illuminate the area.

Jamal slammed into Claude as though tackling a running back. Claude spun around but didn't go down. He thrashed his arms about. One of them connected with Jamal's head, momentarily dazing him.

I ran to Colin and helped him to his feet. Blood streamed down the side of his head.

"Can you walk?" I asked.

He looked shocked. "Where am I? What's going on?"

He had been knocked senseless. I turned in time to see Claude slam Jamal in the chest and send him sprawling to the ground.

Claude closed in on him. Jamal stood up. With a swing of his arm, Claude sent Jamal flying against a tree. The sound of the impact was sickening.

Ricki began to slide down the tree, screaming, "I'm falling!"

Colin took an unsteady step before collapsing to his knees.

Claude would make mincemeat out of us if I didn't do something fast. I left Colin on the ground and sprinted toward Jamal. I waved my hands and shouted to get Claude's attention.

“Hey! Hey! You don’t want him. You want me!” I yelled.

He craned his head around, like an owl turning its head at an impossible angle. He stared at me with his inky eyes. They opened wide with recognition.

“*Yuuuuuuuurrrrggghhhh...*”

Claude lunged at me. I stepped out of the way, drawing him after me. He stumbled a few steps toward me. I backed up, holding the lantern high.

“Ricki!” I yelled. “Take the guys back to the dorm and get help!”

“What are you going to do?” she asked.

“I’m leading this creep away to give you time to help Jamal and Colin,” I said.

“Don’t do it! It’s too dangerous!”

“As soon as it’s clear, get them out of here,” I shouted.

I lowered the lantern and aimed it at the rotting man. He growled.

“You know who I am, don’t you? I’m the one who kicked over the gravestone. That’s right. Come and get me, if you want to get your revenge.”

Claude lunged at me again. I stumbled back, nearly tripping on a root, but I kept my balance. I turned and ran toward the edge of the clearing, running fast enough to keep out of his grasp but slow enough not to lose him.

He moaned as he stumbled toward me, picking up speed with every step. I led him through the trees toward the site of his grave. As long as he followed me, Ricki and the others would have a chance to survive the night. I couldn’t say the same for me.

Chapter Thirteen

The lantern blasted the darkness away as I ran between the trees. I had to retrace my steps to the gravesite. Behind me Claude crashed through the brush. Did this guy ever run out of steam? I hoped I had given the others enough time to get away. If they could get to the school and let the staff know what I was up against, help would come. I had to hold out until someone found me.

But how was anyone going to find me? None of the kids had seen the gravesite, and the woods were vast. I hoped the lantern light would guide people to me. But Jamal and Ricki would have to find the staff at this late hour. And I wondered what had happened to the other students. They hadn't answered their phones. Were they still in the forest, or had Claude found them?

These thoughts filled me with dread as I ran through the woods. Finally I stumbled toward an area that looked familiar. A few branches were broken off, as if someone had been cutting a path through the dense brush. Was this Claude's work? I followed the new path until I saw Claude's gravestone. I had found the cemetery.

A few steps farther, I saw the rough hole in front of Claude Dubois's gravestone. Empty. My breath caught. I was right! Claude Dubois *had* crawled out. Now I had to find a way to make him go back in.

Claude moaned as he shambled toward me. I circled around the area, keeping the gravestone between us. I had to step over the hole to avoid falling in. He lunged at me, but I stepped back out of his reach.

I thought about what Pru had said about the Dubois family and the evil force that had driven Claude to jump. Then there was Jamal's story about the strange feeling he'd had when he neared the graves. Was all of this connected? Why had Claude come out now?

Claude lunged for me again, nearly grabbing hold of my arm as I stepped over the hole in the ground. I pulled away and stumbled backward, tripping on the fallen gravestone that I had kicked over. I landed hard on my back. I gasped for air, trying to catch my breath.

Claude had begun to advance on me when a shadowy figure slammed into him. I aimed the lantern up. It was Jamal. He was bloodied and bruised, but he had somehow found us.

“Jamal!” I screamed. “Get away. He’s too strong.”

Jamal grunted as he held back his attacker. “I’m buying you time to get away. Go!”

But he was fighting a losing battle. Claude was too powerful. He grabbed Jamal’s arm and yanked hard. *Snap.*

Jamal’s screams cut through the night. I cringed at the sound. When I looked up, Jamal’s left arm dangled uselessly by his side as Claude took the boy’s head and began to squeeze.

“Aaaaaaaaaaggggggghhhhhh!” Jamal howled.

I tried to scramble up to save Jamal, but I froze when Claude peered at me, still gripping Jamal’s head in his hands. No. He wasn’t looking at me. He was staring at the grave marker I had kicked over.

I held the lantern high enough to light up the etching on the stone. The writing on the stone read

Margaret Dubois

Loving wife

The gravestone I had knocked over wasn't just any marker. It belonged to the woman Claude Dubois had loved more than anything. Was he upset that I had kicked over her gravestone? Was that the reason he had crawled out of his own grave? To make me pay for knocking down his wife's gravestone? I didn't know, but I knew I couldn't keep running forever. I had no idea when or if anyone was coming to help. I had to do something.

I lowered the lantern to the ground, dug my fingers under Margaret's gravestone and heaved it up. Claude growled but didn't move from his spot. I struggled to lift the stone up and erect.

"I'm sorry, Mr. Dubois," I said. "Let me make this right."

He cocked his head to one side but didn't move. He watched as I heaved the gravestone into position. It was shaky, but his wife's marker was back up and where it belonged. Then the thing toppled back. *Thunk!*

It had struck something hard. I scrambled around to see what it was. I shoved Margaret's stone sideways across a hard, moss-covered rock. No, not a rock. A stone slab set in the ground. Not standing upright like Margaret's grave, but placed in between her marker and Claude's.

"*Unnnnggggh*," Claude moaned. He let go of Jamal's head, letting him slump to the ground. Jamal was out cold.

I lowered the lantern and wiped away the rest of the moss. The slab said

Cora Dubois

Three hearts forever

Claude began to crawl toward me.

"What do you want from me?" I screamed.

Claude climbed to his feet and towered over me. I could smell him from where I knelt. I held my breath, expecting the worst. I had done what I could to restore his wife's gravestone, but this wasn't what he had wanted. I felt a pit in my stomach. The air grew thick and heavy like an invisible giant's fist was squeezing all around me. The hunger.

Then Claude put one foot in the hole of his grave and began to climb in. He never took his eyes off me. No, he never took his eyes off his wife's gravestone. He lowered himself into the hole until all I could see was the top of his body.

Then he reached over and grabbed Jamal's leg and began to drag him toward the grave.

"No! No! What are you doing? Let go of him," I pleaded.

He ignored me, dragging Jamal closer to the hole.

"Stop!" I screamed.

Jamal was inches from going into the hole with Claude. I had to act now. There was only one thing to do. I summoned my strength and heaved Margaret's gravestone upright, then pushed it toward Claude.

Inch by inch. It was a race to see who would get to the hole first, Jamal or me.

Claude turned to see what I was doing, but it was too late. With one last burst of energy, I pushed the stone toward Claude and let go. It crashed down on Claude, driving him into the hole. *Crunch.*

He stopped moving. I grabbed Jamal's right arm and hauled him out of Claude's reach. I froze as I saw Claude's rotting hand twitch and move. Slowly it slipped down into the hole.

Silence.

It was over. I had beaten the zombie. Or driven back the ghost. Whatever it was, it was done. I plopped on the ground and began to chuckle. It was a nervous laugh. I couldn't help it. If I didn't laugh, I would cry. The long night was finally over.

I leaned back on my hands and inhaled the cool night air. Suddenly I felt something wrap around my wrist. I tried to pull away, but the grip was icy and tight. I stared at a rotting woman's hand clutching my wrist. Margaret's other hand burst free from the dirt and latched on to my arm.

I tried to escape, but she was powerful. Her skeletal head emerged from the grave, her eyes fixed on me. She opened her mouth, and worms spewed out. Then she pulled me toward the hole. I couldn't break free. I screamed for help, but Jamal was hurt, and no one knew where we were.

Her bony hand on my wrist burned as it scraped a chunk of my flesh away. With my free hand, I clawed at her face, trying to shake her off me. Her face was caked with dirt and worms. Her grip was unshakable. She was dragging me into the grave.

I stopped clawing and reached for something to smash down on Margaret's head. Just a few feet away, I saw a large rock, the chunk that had broken off the gravestone when I'd first kicked it. I reached for the rock, but it was too far away, and I was inching closer to the hole. I stretched out my leg and hooked the rock with my foot, dragging it toward me until I could grab it. Then, with one last burst of strength, I raised the rock and smashed it against Margaret's arms.

She didn't make a sound, but the impact forced her to let go. I scrambled away and climbed to my knees. I hoisted the rock over my head and smashed it down on her skull, driving her into the grave. Then I dropped the rock and staggered over to Jamal.

He groaned, "My arm. I think it's broken."

I gently helped him to his feet. He moaned in pain when his broken arm brushed against me. I looked back at the still forms of Claude and Margaret Dubois, half in and half out of their graves. Would they move again? I didn't want to stick around to find out.

"Let's get out of here, Jamal."

"Not going to fight you on that," he grunted.

We limped through the brush, away from the graves. I had found a narrow path that snaked through the trees. The air still felt heavy and charged.

The presence was still with us. I could feel its hunger clutching at my heart. I glanced uneasily at Jamal. He nodded.

"I feel it too," he whispered.

I picked up the pace, wanting to get out of the woods as fast as I could.

Suddenly a shriek cut the night air. I spun around. Jamal groaned in pain.

"That sounded like Pru," I said.

Jamal nodded. "I thought she would have found her way back to the dorm."

"We have to go back," I said, lifting my lantern.

He nodded. We turned around and limped back to the cemetery. The heavy feeling in the air twisted my stomach into knots as we pushed through the brush. I listened for any sound from Pru, but the night air was silent except for my breathing and Jamal's moans of pain.

Finally we were back at the cemetery. Our lantern lit up the area. I froze in horror.

Margaret and Claude Dubois were now out of their graves, one on each side of Pru Cotton. They held her hands and stroked her curly blond hair. Pru's body shook, and her eyes rolled back. She opened her mouth, but no sound came out.

"Let go of her!" I barked.

Neither of them even looked my way. They just held on to Pru's hands and stroked her hair while her body jerked and twitched. I'd started toward them when a bright-green light exploded from Pru's body. I raised my arm to shield my eyes from the flash.

When the glow faded, I lowered my arm. The night air felt lighter now. Gone was the pit in my stomach. The hunger. I scanned the area, but there was no sign of Claude or Margaret Dubois. Just dust swirling around Pru's body, which was curled up on the ground between the gravestones.

Jamal and I shared a look, unable to move for a second.

“What happened?” Jamal asked.

I glanced at Pru’s still form. “I think Claude and Margaret got what they needed.” Slowly I inched toward Pru’s body, holding the lantern high. Her face was pale, and her eyes were open but lifeless.

“Is she okay?” Jamal asked.

I knelt down beside her and put my hand under her nose. No sign of breathing. I looked back at Jamal and shook my head.

“She’s dead, but I think...I think the Dubois took her soul,” I said. But why? I wondered. If Cora’s grave was here, why did they need another soul?

“Where are they?” Jamal asked.

I looked around the gravesite. Dawn’s light began to illuminate the woods. No sign of either Claude or Margaret Dubois. Just dust hanging in the air above Cora Dubois’s grave.

Chapter Fourteen

I peeled the cat poster from my dorm-room wall while Ricki crammed her clothes into a suitcase. Two weeks after Pru's death, all the Heartwood students were being sent home. Pru's parents blamed the school for failing to protect their daughter. Other parents said the senior students should have stopped the test. The cops questioned Jamal and me, thinking we'd had something to do with Pru's death.

Jamal and I had tried to tell the real story, but no one believed us. Not the teachers. Not the cops. Not even the other students. We were finally cleared when the medical examiner reported that Pru had suffered a heart attack. No one had a clear explanation for why a teenage girl in good health would have had a heart attack, but I knew the truth. Well, most of it. I had just one nagging question.

Ricki held up her green Heartwood jacket. "Allie, you think they'll shut this place down for good?"

I shrugged. "They have no choice. No students. No school."

She eyed her jacket. "Then I guess I won't need the school uniform," she said, tossing the jacket on the floor.

I left Ricki to finish packing while I headed off to find some answers. I couldn't leave Heartwood without at least trying to find an explanation. Why did Claude and Margaret Dubois need another soul?

I headed down the stairs to the sophomores' dorm rooms to find Jamal. His door was open, and he was hunched over his laptop. His room was a disaster zone. He hadn't even started packing his things.

I knocked on the open door. "Jamal? You find anything?"

He turned. He looked like he hadn't slept in a week. His eyes were sunken, and his hair was a mess. His left arm was in a cast.

"Allie, come over here," he said.

I rushed over to his desk and glanced at the laptop screen. It looked like a record of deaths in the community around Heartwood Academy.

I raised an eyebrow. "What's this?"

"I looked for an announcement of Cora Dubois's death," Jamal explained. "I found one for Margaret Dubois, but nothing about Cora."

"Maybe they didn't report infant deaths back then," I suggested.

He pointed at the screen. "I found three reports of infant deaths in the same year. Their births here, see?" He pointed at a column of names. "Their deaths here. If Cora had died, someone would have recorded it."

"You mean she didn't die at birth?" I asked.

Jamal shook his head. "I don't think Cora ever existed. I went over the Dubois family's records online, and I found some scans of Margaret's letters. She had written a bunch to her sister. Turned out Cora wasn't the first time Margaret had said she was pregnant. She'd had two previous pregnancies, but they both turned out to be false. Phantom pregnancies, I think they're called. The fact that she couldn't have a child wore on her to the point where she told her sister she looked for help from the spirit world. But Margaret said that she only made the spirits angry. In her final letter, she told her sister one of them haunted her to the point where she couldn't go on living."

"She killed herself?" I asked. "Wait. Then why did Claude make up the story about Margaret dying in childbirth?"

"Maybe he didn't want people to know about Margaret losing her mind. Claude knew the Cora story was a lie, but maybe he told it to paint over the truth. Allie, when you kicked her gravestone, it woke Margaret's ghost and her need to have a kid. And Claude had to ease his wife's pain."

I slowly nodded. "His final words were *three hearts forever*. It was a lie."

"Or a promise," Jamal said. "That he was finally able to keep."

"I hope it was enough," I said.

Jamal tilted his head to one side, confused. "They have Pru's soul. What more do they need?"

"You said Margaret had had two previous phantom pregnancies. She thought she had lost three babies."

"No," Jamal said. "Pru's soul was enough. She had to be enough."

The air in the room suddenly grew cold and still. Jamal and I stared at each other. Was it my imagination, or could I hear a woman's voice?

Words echoed in my mind. *Three hearts forever.*

Acknowledgments

Have you ever noticed that when you have a job to do, the task seems easier if you're not alone? I know the stereotype of an author is the image of them sitting alone in their study, penning a manuscript in isolation. In my case, nothing could be further from the truth. There were guides all along my journey. While they might not always be visible to the readers, their impact is evident to me. For all the help I've received putting together this work, I'd like to thank my guides: Michelle Chan, Gabrielle Prendergast, Vivian Sinclair and Wei Wong. I'd also like to give a shout-out to Michael Bell and the Tsukuba International School. My virtual visit to your school gave me the idea for the setting of this novel. Thank you!